For Joshua . . . and bedtimes past F.S.

For my Mum and Dad, thank you for your
endless encouragement, support and love C.C.

First published in the UK in 2017
First published in the USA in 2017
by Faber & Faber Limited
Bloomsbury House, 74–77 Great Russell Street, London WC1B 3DA
and Profile Books, 3 Holford Yard, Bevin Way, London WC1X 9HD
www.profilebooks.com

Designed by Faber and Faber
Printed in Europe
All rights reserved

Text © Francesca Simon, 2017
Illustrations © Charlotte Cotterill, 2017

The rights of Francesca Simon and Charlotte Cotterill to be identified
as author and illustrator of this work respectively have been asserted
in accordance with Section 77 of the Copyright, Designs and
Patents Act 1988

A CIP record for this book is available from the British Library

HB ISBN 978–0571–32871–0
PB ISBN 978–0571–32872–7

2 4 6 8 10 9 7 5 3 1

FSC
www.fsc.org

MIX
Paper from
responsible sources
FSC® C022612

FABER & FABER has published children's books since 1929. Some of our very first publications included *Old Possum's Book of Practical Cats* by T. S. Eliot starring the now world-famous Macavity, and *The Iron Man* by Ted Hughes. Our catalogue at the time said that 'it is by reading such books that children learn the difference between the shoddy and the genuine'. We still believe in the power of reading to transform children's lives.

HACK and WHACK

FRANCESCA SIMON

ILLUSTRATED BY CHARLOTTE COTTERILL

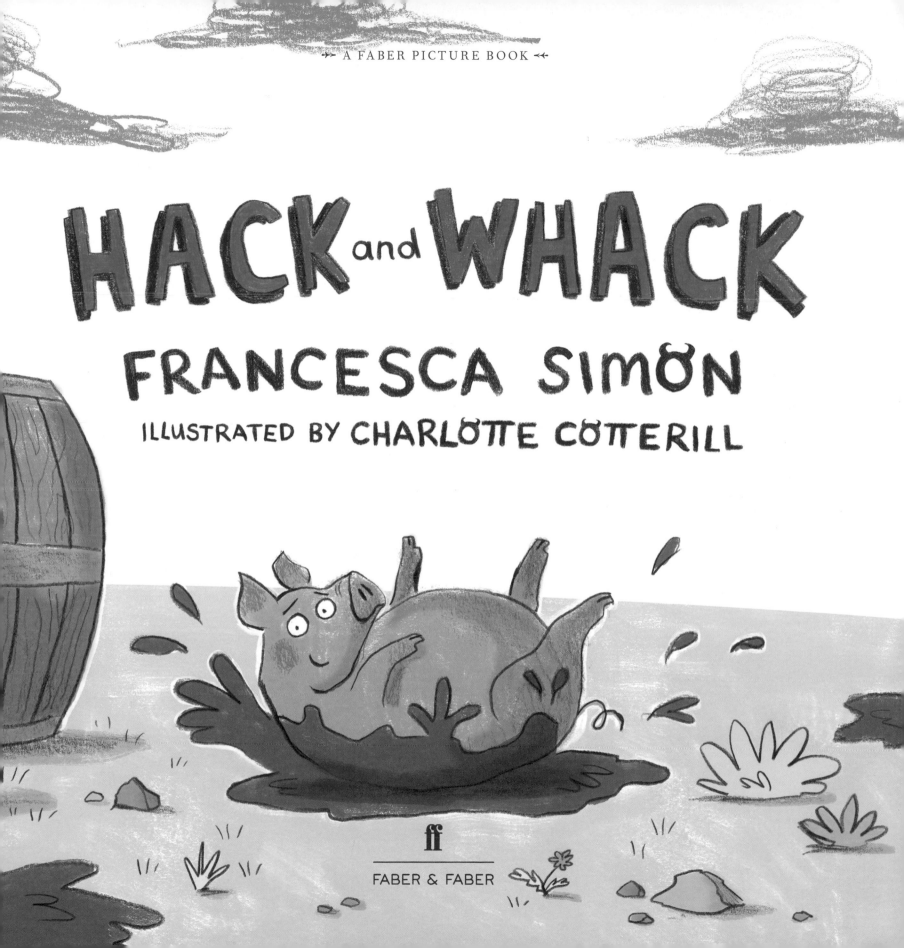

ff

FABER & FABER

...RAMPAGING

CLICKETY...

CLACK

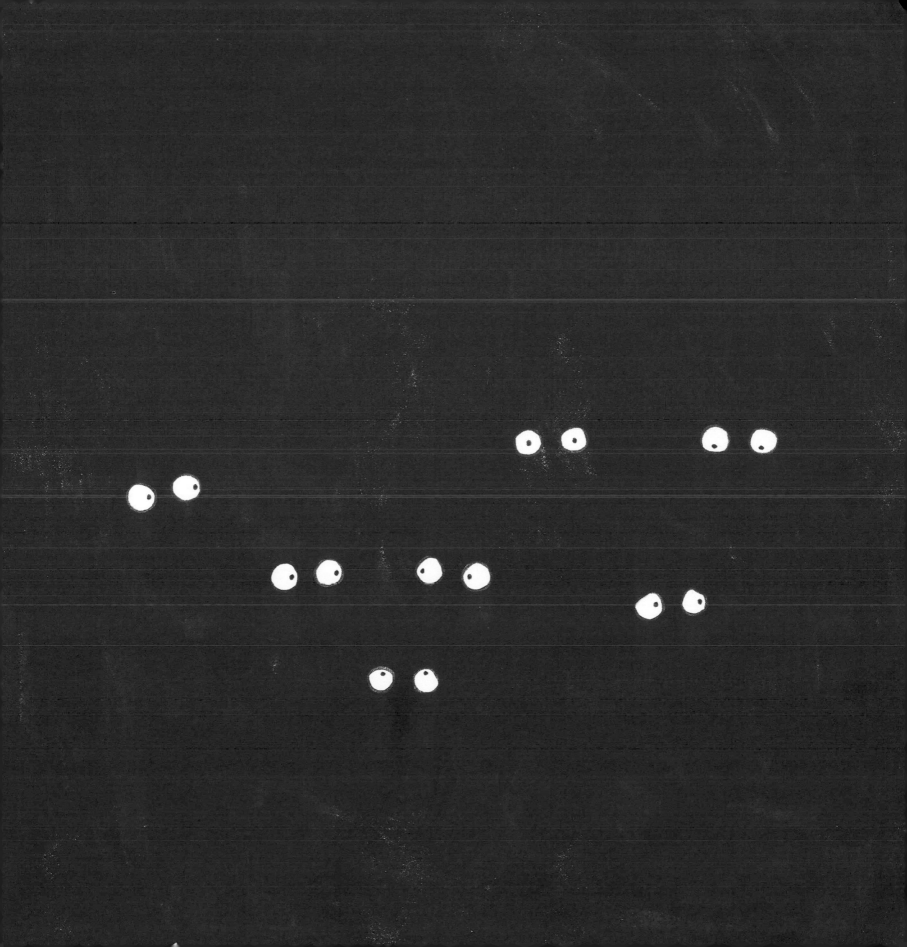

---sleeeeeep!

The End